D1383700

First American Edition 2021
Kane Miller, A Division of EDC Publishing

La Rentrée des animaux
Published in France in 2018 by les Éditions de L'Élan vert
© Éditions de L'Élan vert, 2018

For information contact:
Kane Miller, A Division of EDC Publishing
5402 S 122nd E Ave, Tulsa, OK 74146
www.kanemiller.com
www.usbornebooksandmore.com

Library of Congress Control Number: 2020949036

Manufactured by Regent Publishing Services, Hong Kong China
Printed March 2021 in Shenzhen, Guangdong, China

1 2 3 4 5 6 7 8 9 10
ISBN: 978-1-68464-274-8

Pour Elia, qui va bientôt faire
sa première rentrée à l'école !
Et pour Maryam et Radya !
N. C.

À Madame Danton, ma maîtresse de CM1.
H. L. G.

Noé Carlain
Hervé Le Goff

Back to School

Kane Miller
A DIVISION OF EDC PUBLISHING

The HEDGEHOGS are going back to school.

"Ouch! No pushing!"
"That's sharp!"

The ELEPHANTS are going back to school.

"I don't know why my backpack is so heavy!

It just has my notebook, my pencil case, and my lunch."

The SNAILS
are going back to school.

"Come on, class, a little faster, please."

The CROCODILES are going back to school.

Some are happy, some are nervous, and some are in (crocodile) tears.

"Mom! Come back!"

The BATS
are going back to school.
Everything must be upside down
to be right side up.

"Is everyone here?
Wave your wing
when I call your name."

The WOLVES
are going back to school.

"Everyone must put
their special friend here
during class."

Baa!
Baa!

"Yours looks just like mine!"

The PIGS are going back to school.

Art is first.

"Yours is really good."

"Thanks! I didn't even use a brush!"

The DUCKS are going back to school.

It's time for lunch ...

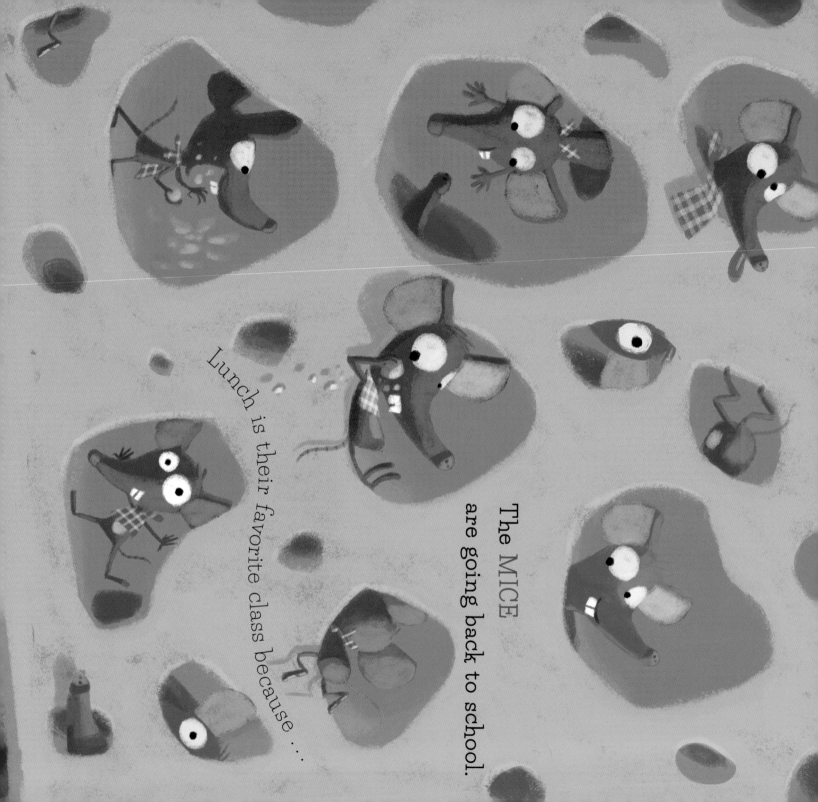

Lunch is their favorite class because ...

The MICE are going back to school.

The BEARS are going back to school.

"How long is nap time?"

"Just another few months."

The RABBITS are going back to school.

"I don't know the answer!"

"Look around – can you see a hint?"

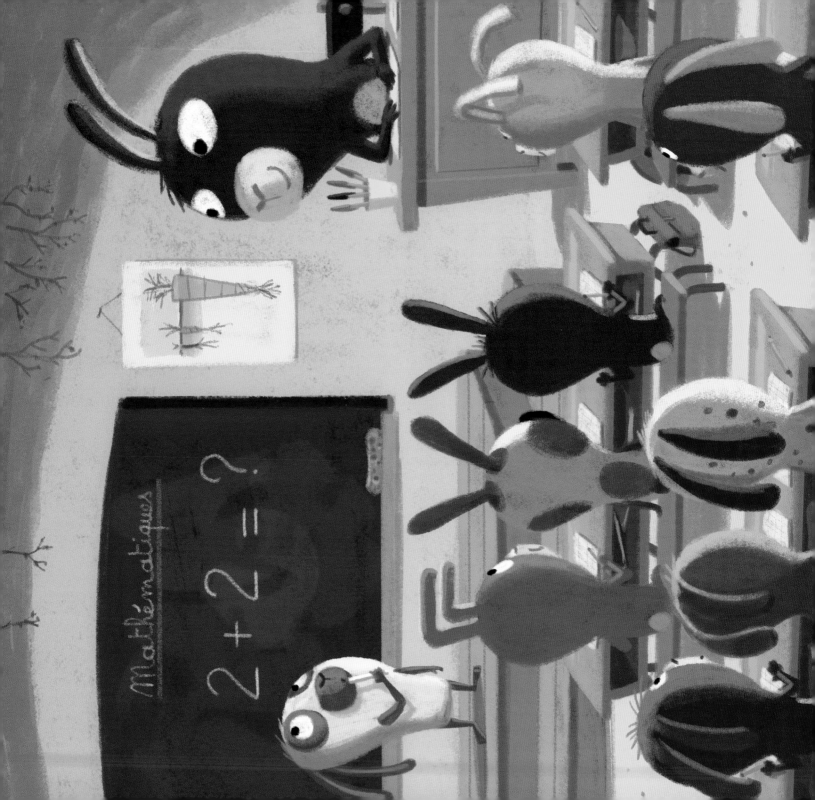

It's already time to go home!

What a great day!

"Do we get to come back tomorrow?"

"I can't wait!"